Tabi's

NINJATASTIC

ABC Adventure

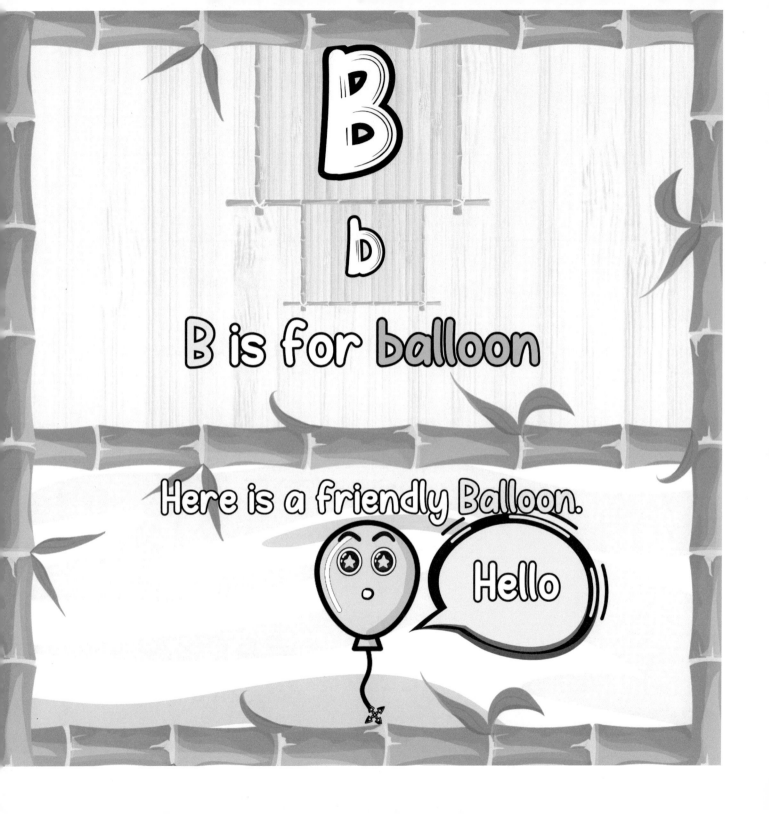

D

d

D is for drink

Tabi has cup of tea in his hand.

When his tea gets warm he takes a drink.

E

e

E is for eye

The arrow is pointing at Tabi's eye.

F
f

F is for food

Look at the yummy food.

H
h

H is for helmet

The arrow is pointing at a helmet.

I

i

I is for ice

Tabi is skating on ice.

K
k

K is for kick

Tabi hit the ball with a powerful kick.

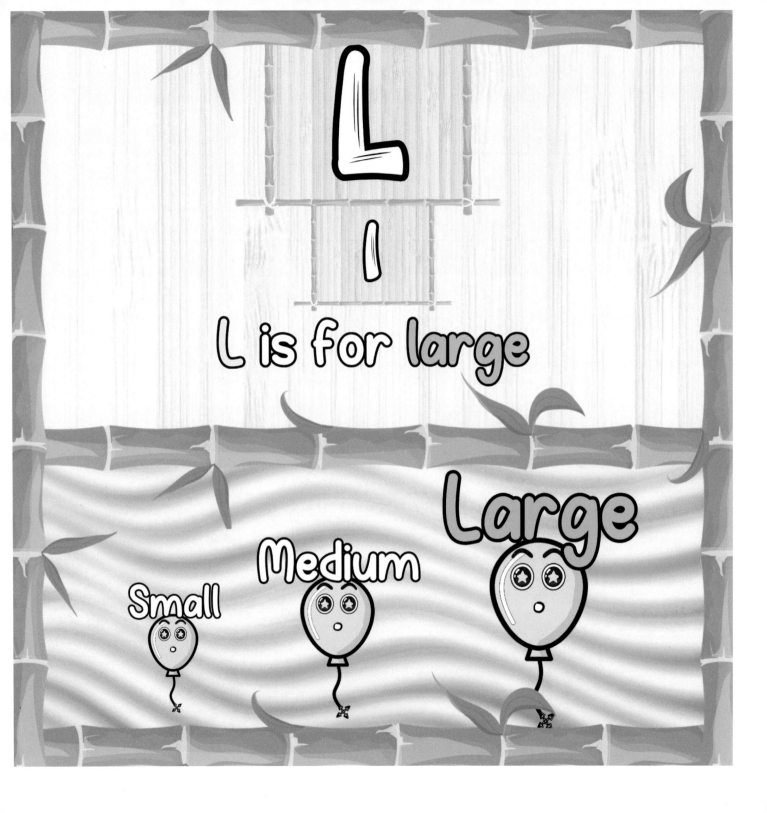

N
n

N is for Ninja

The ninja is throwing his ninja star.

O

o

O is for octopus

Tabi is swimming with an octopus.

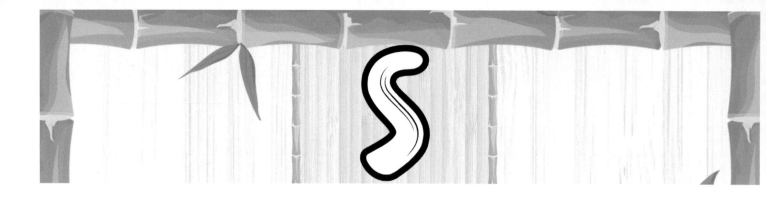

T t

T is for tall

Compared to the little Ninja Tabi looks Tall.

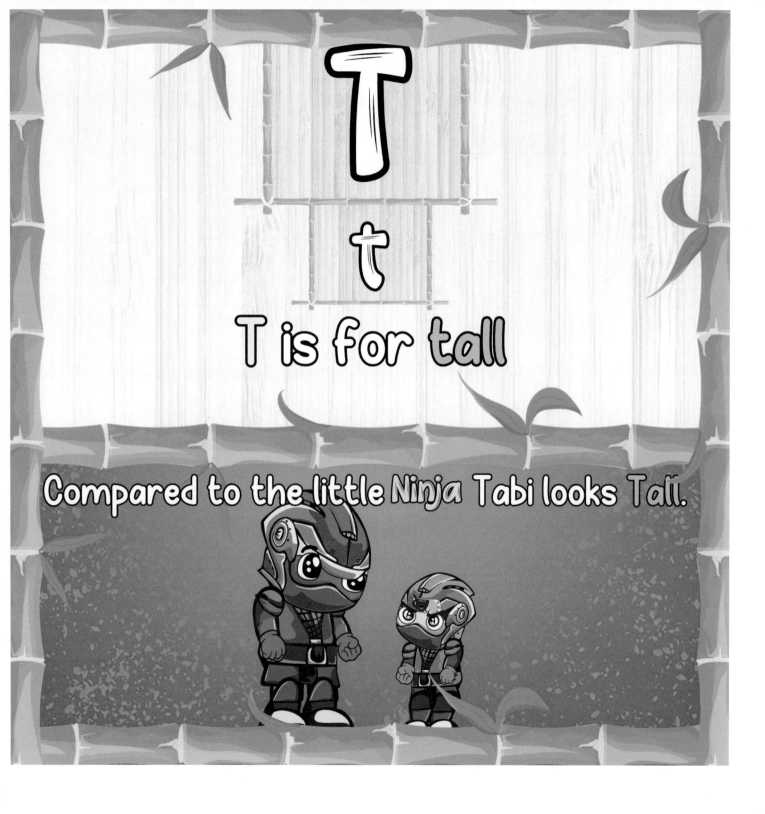

Flip the page upside-down!

U is for upside-down

u

U

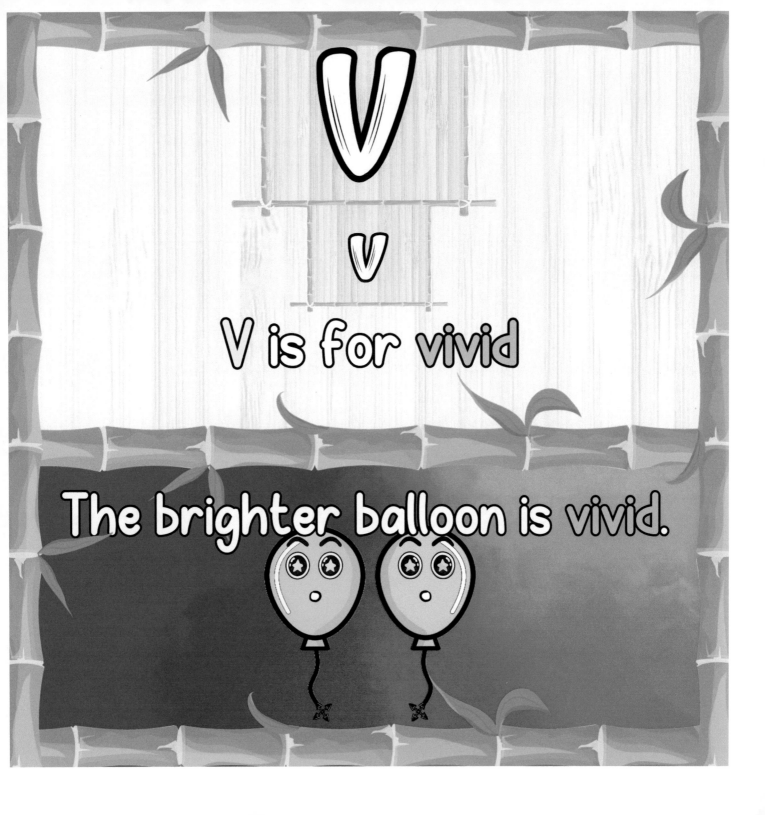

W
w

W is for waffle

Tabi is going to eat the waffle.

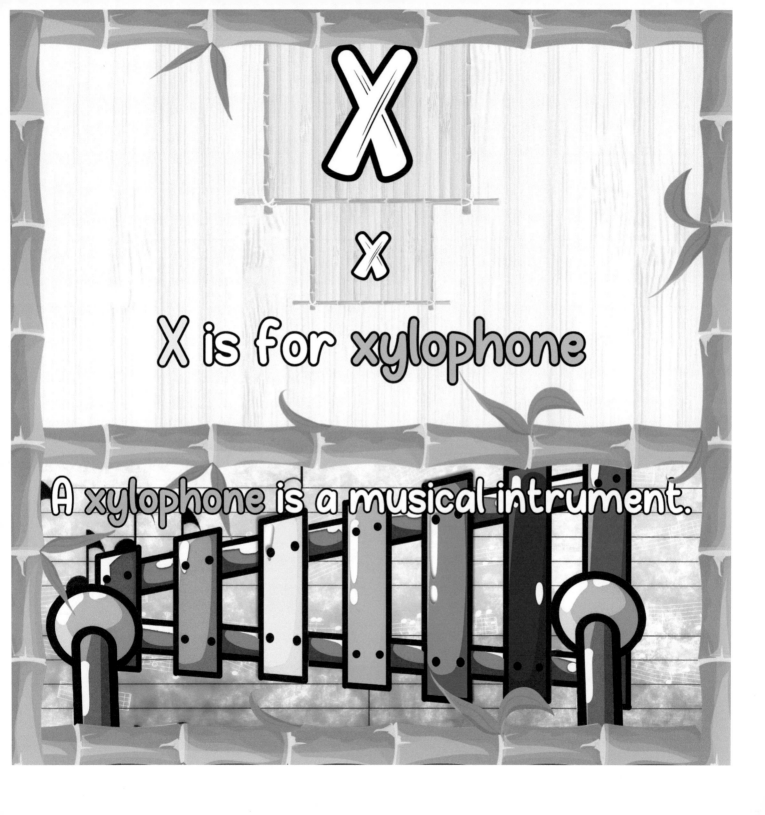

X

x

X is for xylophone

A xylophone is a musical intrument.

To get away from the bomb **Tabi** has to

???
_____

Find the missing word

Eat   Waffle   Run

Tabi is skating on
???
_____

Find the missing word

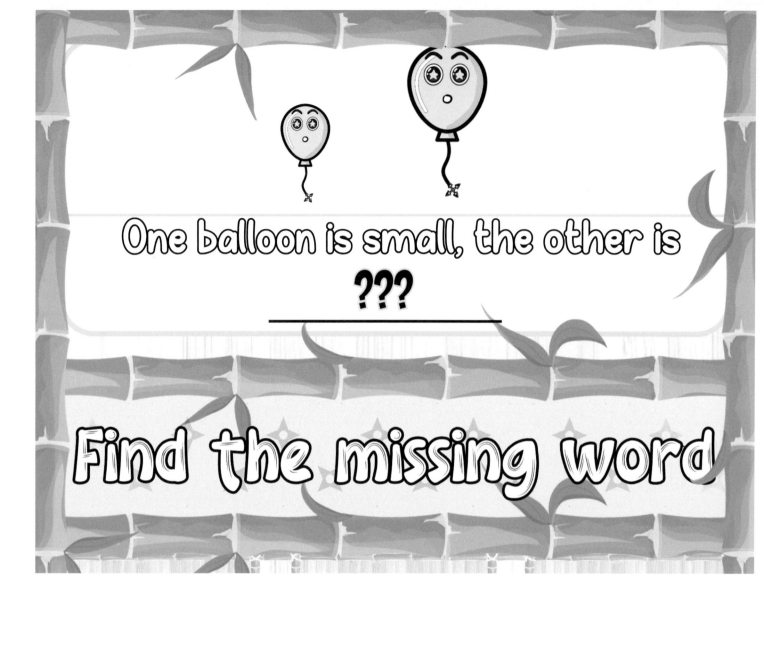

One balloon is small, the other is
???
_____

Find the missing word

Blair got stronger and became **???**

Find the missing word

Octopus Vivid Massive

Blair hit the ball with a powerful

???
_____

Find the missing word

Kick

Ninja

Tall

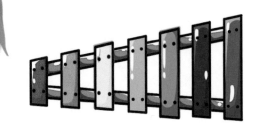

This instrument is called a

???
_____

Find the missing word

Quick   Xylophone   Balloon

The End

Written & Engineered

By

ELIAHNINJA

Eliah Arigbon

Made in United States
Troutdale, OR
05/06/2024

19583318R00021